This book belongs to:

....

....

Retold by Monica Hughes
Illustrated by Andy Catling

Reading consultants: Betty Root and Monica Hughes

Marks and Spencer p.l.c.
PO Box 3339
Chester, CH99 9QS

shop online
www.marksandspencer.com

ISBN 978-1-84461-568-1
Printed in China

Hansel
and Gretel

MARKS &
SPENCER

Helping your child to read

First Readers are closely linked to the National Curriculum. Their vocabulary has been carefully selected from the word lists recommended by the National Literacy Strategy.

Read the story

Read the story
to your child
a few times.

But a bad witch lived in the house.
She put Hansel in a cage.
She made Gretel work for her.

The witch gave Hansel lots of food.
She wanted him to get fat.
"I want to eat you!" said the witch

22

Follow your finger

Run your finger under
the text as you read.
Your child will soon begin to
follow the words with you.

Look at the pictures

Talk about the pictures. They will
help your child to understand the story.

"I want to eat you!" said
the witch.

23

Have a go

Let your child
have a go at
reading the large
type on each
right-hand page.
It repeats a line
from the story.

Join in

When your child is ready,
encourage them to join in with the
main story text. Shared reading is
the first step to reading alone.

Once upon a time there was a little
boy and a little girl.
The little boy was called Hansel.
The little girl was called Gretel.
Hansel and Gretel lived in a cottage
in the woods.

Hansel and Gretel lived in
the woods.

Hansel and Gretel lived with their
father and stepmother.
They were afraid of their stepmother.

Hansel and Gretel were hungry.
"We have no food," said their father.
Their stepmother said,
"Take the children deep into the
woods and leave them there."

"We have no food."

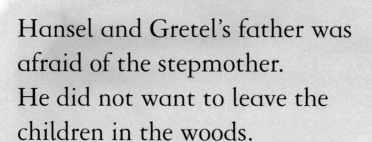

Hansel and Gretel's father was
afraid of the stepmother.
He did not want to leave the
children in the woods.
But he said to Hansel and Gretel,
"Come with me."
And so off they went into the woods.

They went into the woods.

Their father left them deep in
the woods.
Gretel was afraid.
"We are lost," she cried.
"Don't worry," said Hansel.
"I dropped some stones.
We can follow the stones and
go back home."

"Don't worry," said Hansel.

So Hansel and Gretel followed the
stones and went back home.
When their stepmother saw them
she said to their father,
"Take them deep into the woods and
leave them there again."

Then Hansel and Gretel went into the
woods with their father.
He left them deep in the woods again.

Hansel and Gretel went
back home.

Gretel was afraid.

"We are lost," she cried.

"Don't worry," said Hansel.

"I dropped some crumbs.

We can follow the crumbs and
go back home."

But they saw the birds had
eaten the crumbs.

"Don't worry," said Hansel.

Hansel and Gretel were lost deep in
the woods.
Then they saw a little house.
The house was made of sweets.
"We can eat this house," said Hansel.

They saw a little house.

But a bad witch lived in the house.
She put Hansel in a cage.
She made Gretel work for her.

The witch gave Hansel lots of food.
She wanted him to get fat.
"I want to eat you!" said the witch.

"I want to eat you!" said
the witch.

One day the witch wanted to
cook Hansel in a pan.
She made Gretel put a big pan of
water on the fire.

But Gretel pushed the witch.
The witch fell into the big
pan of water.
And that was the end of her.

Gretel pushed the witch.

Then Hansel and Gretel ran home.
When they got home they
saw their father.
Their stepmother had gone.
He was very happy to see Hansel and
Gretel again.

Hansel and Gretel ran home.

Look back in your book.
Can you read these words?

Gretel

Hansel

house

witch

stones

bird

Can you answer these questions?

Where do Hansel
and Gretel live?

Who takes Hansel
and Gretel deep
into the woods?

What does the
witch do to Hansel?

Read Together

Look out for other books in the **First Readers** range (subject to availability):

Fairytale Readers